Linda,

Thank you! ♡

To my Baachan: always remembered, never forgotten. I miss you each and every day.
T & B, I hope this book brings you comfort and understanding.
My rock E, ALWAYS.

ISBN 9780998854557

Library of congress control number:2022909627

Losing a loved one is a very hard thing to go through. Everyone grieves differently and there are so many emotions felt all at once. For me, I actually started writing this book a few years back and when I had only 5 pages left to illustrate, my beloved Baachan (grandma), passed away quite suddenly. She was beautiful and strong for a 99 1/2 year old woman. I was spoiled because for 40 years, I had my grandma in my life and we were super close. I was fortunate enough to help care for her on her last days with us.

My point of telling you this private part of my life is because this happened a year and a half ago now and I just finally finished the last 5 pages. I never got angry during my grieving period. I was very sad and cried a lot when she first passed. Then I eventually felt calm everywhere I went that reminded me of her. I sometimes see beautiful dragonflies and say hello to her because what calms me and makes me happy, is thinking she became that dragonfly to check in on me and say hi. However, the reason it took so long to finish those last few pages was because I simply was not ready to let her go. Finishing the book would mean letting her go and having closure. None of this would make sense to anyone but me because it is not logical to others.

So the key thing I want you to know is that everyone processes and grieves differently and don't let anyone tell you otherwise. There is not a set time you can grieve for. You know yourself the best, when you are ready to move on, move on and cherish those memories always. Please always talk to your parents and communicate with them.

With love,
Masami S.C.

What an amazing aquarium!
Let's say hello to
Brown Bear and Oofie.

Oh dear.
Brown Bear is terribly
upset about something.

Like a good friend should,
Oofie is checking in
with Brown Bear and asking if
she is okay.

We should give Brown Bear a few minutes to calm down.
When she is ready, she will tell us.

Sometimes when we are so upset, it is very hard to **communicate.** Having a good, hard, ugly cry, helps you feel better.

There, you see!
Brown Bear has had a
long, hard cry, and is
ready to talk.

Brown Bear's grandma, has **passed** away. Brown Bear needs us right now. It is hard to find the words to say to a friend when they are upset. Sometimes, just being there for them and sitting in silence, shows you care. Sometimes, you might feel the same as your sad friend and also want to cry.

When a person or pet **departs** our world, it is a very **emotional** time for the loved ones he or she has left behind.

Some people are very sick
before they die.
Some people are healthy but
pass away in their sleep.
Sometimes, accidents
happen and we can also
lose a loved one.

Coping is how we handle our emotions, like when we lose a loved one. Sometimes we are angry. Sometimes, we are so sad that we cannot do anything else, but cry. A lot of times we wish we could hug or kiss them one last time, but cannot. **Coping** is how we move forward without our loved one.

Some people believe in **reincarnation**. Some people believe in the land of the remembered. Some people believe in heaven. Your belief may be different from your friends. What matters most is what brings you peace and makes you calm.

Oofie is correct.
We all have our own religions and beliefs.
When a loved one has departed, believe in what brings you the most comfort and peace.

Always keep an open mind.
That is a great way to live
day to day.

Start a journal and write down lovely memories of your departed loved one. That way, you can always look back and remember when you are older. It is also a good way to help you **grieve.**

Brown Bear should find a stuffed animal or t-shirt she got as a gift from her Mimi. That way, Brown Bear can hug those items whenever she misses Mimi or feels sad. What an excellent way to **cope!**

Grieving takes time, and time will heal you. Do not worry, this pain will eventually pass but the memories will stay with you always.

Brown Bear & Oofie's featured words

Loss of a loved one: When someone you love very much dies.

Communicate: To be able to express what you are feeling to others.

Pass away (passed): Another way to say someone has died.

Depart(s): To leave our world.

Emotional: Happy, sad, disgust, anger, and fear, are the ways your mood changes when feeling these feelings. Sometimes they are really big feelings you cannot control.

Died: The most popular word used for death.

Coping (cope): How you mentally get over unpleasant emotions like losing a loved one.

Reincarnation: A belief that after your body leaves this planet, you get to come back as another person, animal, insect or element.

Grieve (grieving): A healthy and normal reaction to losing a loved one. You don't forget about the loved one, you just find ways to adapt to life without them being there.

Heaven: A belief that once you have died, you go to paradise and live with God.

SOCIAL MEDIA:
INSTAGRAM.COM/MASAMI_SC
FACEBOOK.COM/MASAMISC

WEBSITE:
WWW.MASAMISCBOOKS.COM

EMAIL:
SERENA@MASAMISCBOOKS.COM